# WHERE THERE'S SMOKE . . .

In a daze, Jeremy put his jacket on and walked down the road to the garage.

He found the garage door shut and locked, so he walked around to the smaller side door. It was standing wide open.

A noise came from the back of the garage, where extra parts were stored.

"Jason, is that you?"

There was no answer.

Jeremy slowly moved through the dark garage. There was a strange orange glow in the back. "Hello?"

A figure in black darted past him, knocking him backward into a tool chest.

Jeremy scrambled to his feet. Something didn't smell right.

Smoke!

OTHER YEARLING BOOKS YOU WILL ENJOY:

JOURNEY, *Patricia MacLachlan*
SHILOH, *Phyllis Reynolds Naylor*
MISSING MAY, *Cynthia Rylant*
AWFULLY SHORT FOR THE FOURTH GRADE,
*Elvira Woodruff*
THE SUMMER I SHRANK MY GRANDMOTHER,
*Elvira Woodruff*
HOW TO EAT FRIED WORMS, *Thomas Rockwell*
HOW TO FIGHT A GIRL, *Thomas Rockwell*
BEETLES, LIGHTLY TOASTED, *Phyllis Reynolds Naylor*
MR. TUCKET, *Gary Paulsen*

YEARLING BOOKS are designed especially to entertain and enlighten young people. Patricia Reilly Giff, consultant to this series, received her bachelor's degree from Marymount College and a master's degree in history from St. John's University. She holds a Professional Diploma in Reading and a Doctorate of Humane Letters from Hofstra University. She was a teacher and reading consultant for many years, and is the author of numerous books for young readers.

# THUNDER VALLEY

A YEARLING BOOK J.R. Clarke

Published by
Bantam Doubleday Dell Books for Young Readers
a division of
Bantam Doubleday Dell Publishing Group, Inc.
1540 Broadway
New York, New York 10036

ISBN: 0-440-41220-X

Series design: Barbara Berger

Interior illustration by Michael David Biegel

Printed in the United States of America

January 1998

OPM   10   9   8   7   6   5   4   3   2   1

Dear Readers:

Real adventure is many things—it's danger and daring and sometimes even a struggle for life or death. From competing in the Iditarod dogsled race across Alaska to sailing the Pacific Ocean, I've experienced some of this adventure myself. I try to capture this spirit in my stories, and each time I sit down to write, that challenge is a bit of an adventure in itself.

You're all a part of this adventure as well. Over the years I've had the privilege of talking with many of you in schools, and this book is the result of hearing firsthand what you want to read about most—power-packed adventure and excitement.

You asked for it—so hang on tight while we jump into another thrilling story in my World of Adventure.

Gary Paulsen

# THUNDER VALLEY

# CHAPTER 1

Fourteen-year-old Jeremy Parsons waited at the top of Sawtooth Ridge. This was his favorite run and his favorite time of day. The sun had almost gone down and the last of the stragglers had found their way off the slopes and were now sitting by the fire inside his grandfather's ski lodge, sipping from mugs of hot chocolate.

Jeremy pulled his ski goggles down over his brown eyes and got ready. Inside his head, he heard the voice of the sportscaster:

*And now, ladies and gentlemen, we have the*

*newcomer, Jeremy Parsons, competing in the downhill event against World Cup champion and Olympic gold medalist Jean-Claude Killy. Jeremy's getting into position . . . and he's off!*

Jeremy lunged from the edge and plummeted down the slope. The wind whipped powdery snow up against his red cheeks. He swung around a dangerous stand of pine trees and then over a series of bumps. Everything was a blur. All he could think about was the finish line. At the bottom he skidded to a stop, turned, and breathlessly looked back up at the mountain.

Jean-Claude Killy had been a champion skier back in the 1960s. But he was Jeremy's all-time favorite skier—and the one Jeremy always raced in his imagination.

"Did you beat him this time?"

Jeremy spun around and found himself looking into the face of his mirror image, his twin brother, Jason. Everyone said they looked exactly alike—the same curly blond hair, the same scattering of freckles. But there were some things about them that were definitely not alike. The way Jason loved to play practical jokes, for example.

Jeremy slid past his brother. "As usual, I have no idea what you're talking about."

"Sure." Jason folded his arms. "I watched you come off Sawtooth. You were racing against Jean-Claude like you used to when we were kids."

"So? What if I was?"

Jason's eyes twinkled with mischief. "Oh, never mind. I just came up here to tell you I finished checking the other trails. Looks like everything's all right."

Jeremy felt a twinge of guilt. It had been his turn to check the trails and make sure all the skiers were in. Jason was only supposed to check the lifts. Jeremy ran his hand through his hair sheepishly. "Thanks. I'll take your turn tomorrow."

"No problem. Oh, one other thing. Grandma wants both of us to meet her in the lodge lobby when we're done."

"In the lodge?" Jeremy raised one eyebrow suspiciously. "Why not at the house?"

Jason shrugged. His brown eyes were wide and his face was the picture of innocence.

Jeremy stepped out of his bindings and

hoisted his skis and poles onto his shoulder. "It must really be important if she wants to talk to both of us."

"I'm sure it is." Jason followed his brother down the well-worn path to the Thunder Valley Ski Lodge. Their grandfather had started the lodge more than thirty years earlier. Back then, the lodge was only a one-room log cabin and a rope tow that ran off a gasoline engine to haul the skiers to the top of the trail. It had grown into one of the finest small resorts in the country.

Jeremy and Jason were living at the lodge to help out this ski season. Their grandfather had broken his hip in a skiing accident, and their grandmother had asked the boys' parents to let them stay for the winter. They would be tutored at the lodge. Since their parents would be traveling in Europe for most of the season anyway, they'd decided to let the boys stay.

Jason jumped up onto the wooden porch of the ski lodge and held the door open for his brother. Jeremy stepped inside, and the people sitting around the fireplace immediately stopped talking. He shifted uncomfortably and leaned his skis against the wall.

Suddenly the room erupted with clapping and cheers. One of the college students walked over and slapped Jeremy on the back. "Way to go, Champ."

A pretty girl in a pink ski suit called out, "Can I have your autograph?"

Jeremy gave his brother a questioning look. "What's all this about? I thought you said Grandma wanted us."

Jason shrugged again. A little girl with long black hair pulled on Jeremy's pants leg. "Is it really true that you just raced against a world champion skier and won?"

Jeremy's face grew warm. He turned to his brother and mouthed the words, "I'm going to kill you." Then he turned back to the small crowd, smiled, and bowed. "Thank you. Thank you. But no applause is necessary—just throw money."

Immediately he was barraged with gloves, ski masks, and even a snow boot. He ducked as the boot came at him. It sailed past and walloped

Jason right between the eyes, knocking him back a few steps.

Jeremy laughed. "Serves you right. Looks like your little joke backfired on you."

Jason rubbed his forehead and grumbled. "That wasn't supposed to happen. Next time . . ."

"Next time?" Jeremy picked up the boot and started for him.

Jason held up his hands and backed toward the door. "Hey, you know me. I was just kidding." He slid through the door, leaving it open a crack.

The door slammed shut just as the boot smashed into it.

# CHAPTER 2

The next day, the boys hurried through their morning routines and then went back to the house for a quick breakfast.

"Your grandfather is in one of his moods this morning." A thin woman with gray-streaked hair pulled into a severe bun set a platter of bacon on the dining room table. "Your grandmother, poor thing, is in there now trying to calm him down."

The boys could hear loud voices coming from their grandparents' bedroom.

Jason scooped a large portion of bacon onto his plate. "What's the problem this time, Lila?"

Lila had been hired a few months earlier by their grandmother as housekeeper and part-time nurse for their grandfather. Lila had already threatened to quit several times because of their grandfather's outbursts. But each time, their gentle grandmother had persuaded her to stay, at least until Grandpa was well again.

Lila folded her hands and looked primly at Jason over the top of her horn-rimmed glasses. "It's this place. Mr. Parsons is having some sort of financial trouble." Then, as if she'd said too much, she turned on her heel and went back into the kitchen.

Jeremy slid out of his chair. "I'll go back and see if there's anything I can do."

"Good idea." Jason reached for the platter again. "And I'll take care of your share of the bacon."

Jeremy met his grandmother coming out of the bedroom. "Is everything okay?"

Grace Parsons sighed and moved a short strand of white hair out of her face. "His hip is bothering him. But it's more than that. He claims that receipts are down and the lodge isn't bringing in money the way it should."

Jeremy frowned. "How can that be? We're packed with customers. David even asked Jason and me if we'd take over teaching the beginners' class because he's swamped."

"I know, dear. I tried to tell your grandfather. Maybe you can convince him not to worry."

"I'll do my best." Jeremy knocked lightly on the bedroom door.

A voice from inside growled, "What do you want?"

"It's me, Grandpa, Jeremy. Can I come in?"

"And why in the name of great Jehoshaphat couldn't you come in? I won't eat you, you know."

Jeremy opened the door, poked his head in, and grinned. "Are you sure? Have you had breakfast yet?"

"Very funny. Get in here, Twin, and tell me what's going on out there in the real world."

Papers and account ledgers covered every available spot on the old-fashioned feather bed. The big man was propped up on several pillows and had obviously been going over the lodge's record books. His glasses had slipped down his long, pointed nose. He pushed them up with one finger. "Pull up that chair over there, Twin."

George Parsons had always been an athletic man. He was sixty-two and, until his accident, had still been able to beat most of the college kids down Sawtooth. Being confined to a bed was torture for him.

Jeremy grabbed the desk chair, flipped it around, and straddled it. He studied his grandfather's face. It looked tired and worried. "What's going on, Grandpa?"

"You want the straight skinny or a cover-up?"

Jeremy tried not to laugh at the way his grandfather talked. Sometimes he had to go to his grandmother to get the things Grandpa said interpreted.

Jeremy cleared his throat. "Give it to me straight, Grandpa."

"Thunder Valley is in trouble. Since I've been laid up, strange things have been happening."

"Like what?"

"This." Grandpa pushed his glasses up again and reached for a bankbook. "Every couple of weeks I send a deposit to the bank. But when I get the statement back it doesn't match the amount I recorded."

"Have you called the bank?" Jeremy asked.

"I called them. Bunch of ninnies. They swear up and down that their records match to the penny the money I've been sending in."

"That's weird. Maybe you should have someone double-check your figures."

"Check my figures?" George Parsons's face turned purple and his voice grew loud. "That's just what your grandmother said. She thinks my pain medication has addled my brain. I'll have both of you know that I've been doing my own bookkeeping for thirty years. I don't need anybody to baby-sit me."

Jeremy decided to change the subject. "You said there were other things going on. What are they?"

His grandfather let out a weary breath and leaned back on the pillows. "Remember the new double chairlifts I said I wanted to install this year on the bunny slope?"

Jeremy nodded.

"I ordered them last season. They're still not

here. Every time I call the company, they insist they never received payment."

"Don't you have a receipt or something to show you paid?"

Jeremy's grandfather shook his head. "It's the darnedest thing. I always keep a careful record of things like this. Somehow it's turned up missing."

Jeremy stood and pushed the chair back under the desk. "I wouldn't worry so much, Grandpa. All these things can be straightened out. In the meantime, Jason and I are keeping an eye on things. We're busier than last year. By the end of the month, you should be rich."

"Thanks for helping out, Twin. I feel better knowing that someone I can trust is out there."

# CHAPTER 3

"What does Grandma think?" Jason wrapped a bright yellow scarf around his neck and followed Jeremy to the snack bar.

"She doesn't know what to think—or do. She wanted to hire an accountant but Grandpa won't give up doing the books."

A friendly face appeared at the snack window. "What'll it be, gents?"

"Hi, Corky." Jeremy took off one of his gloves and rested his skis against the building. "How about a hot chocolate?"

"Hot chocolate it is." The redheaded young

man looked at Jason. "I suppose you want your usual—cola mixed with grape slush?"

Jason nodded. "It's the breakfast drink of champions."

"Right." After a minute Corky handed them their drinks. As he did, the sun flashed on a small gold medallion he wore around his neck. Jeremy found himself staring at it. It was an emblem in the shape of an upside-down V with a bold black line through the middle: ⋏.

Jeremy started to ask what it was, but Corky noticed him looking at it. He hastily tucked it inside his turtleneck. "It's a fraternity thing from school. Anything else I can get for you guys?"

"No thanks, Corky." Jason took a long pull on his drink and belched. "We're working men. See you later."

"That was strange." Jeremy led the way to the beginners' practice area.

"What was strange? I always burp after I drink one of these. They're practically lethal."

"Not you, doofwad—Corky. He acted like he didn't want me to see his necklace."

"Maybe it's secret. You know, some of those

fraternities have passwords and stuff that they don't want anybody else to know."

"Maybe . . ."

Jason tossed his cup into a nearby trash can. "Speaking of stuff nobody knows, did you finish your assignments for Mr. Stern? He'll be here this afternoon to check up on us."

"I finished yesterday. It wasn't hard. Mr. Stern's a pretty good teacher."

"I'll say. And the best part is, he only comes around twice a week."

They rounded the corner of the building and came face to face with David Watts, the ski instructor. He had an angry look on his face. "Okay, what's going on around here? Your grandfather could have at least told me in person."

The twins looked at each other, confused. Jeremy spoke first. "What are you talking about, David? We were just on our way to get this morning's list of students."

"What students?" The handsome athlete shoved a crumpled piece of paper at him.

Jeremy smoothed it out and read aloud, " 'All skiing lessons have been discontinued until further notice, due to lack of a certified instructor.' "

"I don't get it," Jason said. "Aren't you a certified instructor?"

"Take a look at this." David gave Jason a pink slip of paper. "It was in my mailbox yesterday."

Jason skimmed through the letter. "I don't believe it. Grandpa wouldn't do something like this."

"What?" Jeremy grabbed the letter from his brother. "This says Grandpa has accused you of improper behavior with the students and demands your immediate resignation."

"I can read," the instructor snarled. "After six years, he could have at least had the decency to tell me to my face! And what does he mean by 'improper behavior'? I've *never* done anything improper—I just come in and *teach*!"

Jeremy shook his head. "Let me talk to Grandpa, David. There has to be some kind of mistake."

"You bet there is." David Watts stuffed the two notices into his pocket and stomped off toward the lodge. "And your grandfather's the one who made it."

# CHAPTER 4

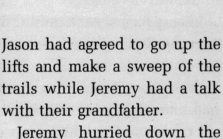

Jason had agreed to go up the lifts and make a sweep of the trails while Jeremy had a talk with their grandfather.

Jeremy hurried down the path to the log house. But he stopped dead in his tracks. Parked in the front yard by the mailbox was an ambulance with its lights flashing. Two emergency medical technicians were carrying a stretcher off the porch. Jeremy dropped his skis and started running.

He met his grandmother in the yard. Her eyes were red from crying. "Thank goodness you're here, Jeremy. You and Jason have got to run

things for a while. Your grandpa has had . . .
another accident. We're taking him to the hospital. I'll call you as soon as I know anything."
One of the EMTs helped her into the ambulance.

"Wait! What kind of accident? Is he gonna be
okay?"

But the ambulance doors closed and the
driver sped away, leaving Jeremy staring in the
middle of the road.

Jeremy turned back toward the house and saw
Lila standing by a window. He raced up onto
the porch and flew inside. Lila was pretending
to be busy straightening the chairs the EMTs
had moved to get the stretcher out.

"What's wrong with my grandfather, Lila?"

The woman stiffened. "I don't think it's my
place to say." She started to walk toward the
kitchen.

Jeremy caught her arm. "I want to know."

Lila's chin went up. "Very well. If you insist.
Your grandfather has attempted suicide."

Jeremy's hand fell away from her arm. He col-
lapsed onto the nearest chair. "That can't be

right. Grandpa had everything to live for. He loves this place. . . ."

"This place is precisely the reason." Lila pulled her sweater around her. "Your grandmother found him passed out in the bedroom. An empty bottle of medicine was in one hand and an overdrawn bank statement was in the other."

The front door burst open. "What's going on?" Jason demanded. "Somebody told me there was an ambulance down here."

Jeremy quietly explained what Lila had told him. Jason closed his eyes and fell onto the sofa. "I don't believe it. Is he gonna be all right?"

"Grandma said she'd call when she found out anything." Jeremy stood up and took a deep breath. "In the meantime, we have a ski lodge to run. Grandma and Grandpa are counting on us."

# CHAPTER 5

Jeremy asked Lila to find him the second his grandmother called. Then he made a list of things that had to be done before the day was over. The first thing on the list was to rehire David Watts as ski instructor. Jason was put in charge of patrolling the slopes, and Jeremy took over the running of the lodge itself.

Jeremy talked to the cafeteria manager and the desk clerk and made arrangements to put the day's income into the lodge's safe. Then he went back to the house to sort out the papers his grandfather had left lying all over his bedroom.

He almost stopped and knocked on the bedroom door, forgetting Grandpa wasn't there. Feeling like an intruder, he pushed the door open.

The room was spotless.

There was no sign that his grandfather had ever been looking at bank statements or account ledgers or anything else. The bed was made up. Not a thing was out of place.

Jeremy turned and almost ran into Lila. Her arms were folded across her chest. "I thought it might be less painful for your grandmother if the room was straightened up when she returned."

"How do you know she's returning? Did she call?"

"Just a few moments before you came in. I tried to reach you at the lodge but they said you'd already left."

"That's okay. What did she say? How is he?"

"Your grandfather has regained consciousness. He doesn't seem to be permanently damaged and the doctors think he will be all right with some rest. Mrs. Parsons is coming home to get some clothing and personal items and then she plans to return to the hospital."

Jeremy sighed with relief, then remembered why he was in the room. "Lila, where did you put all the papers and account books Grandpa had scattered around in here? I want to look at them."

"*You?* Do you think that's wise?"

Jeremy's eyebrows came together in a sharp frown. "My grandmother left me in charge. If I can do anything to help, I'm going to. So where did you put the books?"

Lila unfolded her arms and moved silently down the hallway. "I'll get them for you."

The telephone on the nightstand rang. Jeremy moved around the bed and picked it up. When he did, he realized that someone else had already answered it. He heard a man's voice speaking in a strange monotone.

". . . like lambs to the slaughter. For everything there is a season. The timetable remains the same."

There was no response, only the click of a telephone being hung up. But the other person didn't hang up. Jeremy could hear breathing on the line. As quietly as he could, he put the receiver back in the cradle and moved to the edge of the bed.

In a few minutes Lila appeared with a cardboard box. She placed it on the bed, watching him the whole time. "Here are the things you asked for." Her black eyes darted to the phone beside the bed and then back to him.

Jeremy felt an edge in the room, a change in the air. "Thank you, Lila. I'll just take these to my room and have a look." He picked up the box and moved past her.

"Would you like me to help you, Jeremy? I could explain how bank ledgers work and so forth."

"No thanks. My brother and I have a paper route and a lawn service back home. We keep all our own records. I'm sure I'll catch on."

Jeremy felt Lila's eyes on his back all the way down the hall. But when he looked around, she was gone. He whispered to himself, "Man, you've got to get a grip."

An hour later, Jeremy and Justin's room looked worse than their grandfather's had. Jeremy had pored over every single item in the box. His grandfather had been right about one thing. The initial receipts did not match those the bank had sent back. All the statements were short.

"Boy, what a morning." Jason shuffled through the door, tossed his jacket at a hook on the wall, and crashed on the bottom bunk. "The Thompson brothers started a snowball fight in the beginners' class. A man who never skied before in his life got off the lift at the top of the hardest slope and had to be carried back down by the ski patrol. And then, to top it all off, some stupid kids changed all the trail markers. It's been total chaos all morning. I'm ready for lunch."

"When are you *not* ready for lunch?" Jeremy teased.

Jason threw a pillow at him, knocking one of the piles of paper over. "What's all this stuff?"

Jeremy explained what he was doing and how nothing added up. He also told his brother about the strange phone call. "What do you make of it?"

"I've always thought there was something

weird about Lila—the way she just appears and disappears. It's not normal."

"Your lunch is on the table." Lila was standing in the doorway with her arms folded.

Jeremy wondered how much of their conversation she'd heard. He searched her face but could find no expression there.

Jason bolted for the door. "Food, at last."

Lila moved to let him pass. She looked back at Jeremy. "Are you coming?"

He stood up. "I'll be there in a minute. Oh, and Lila?"

"Yes."

"Don't bother cleaning up in here. I'm still working. I'll straighten up when I'm done."

Jeremy eased past her and headed for the kitchen. He shot a look over his shoulder. This time he caught Lila staring at him with an almost angry glare, but the look changed so suddenly he wasn't positive he'd even seen it.

Lila was smiling. "Is there something you want, Jeremy?"

"I . . . no. Nothing."

"Then I suggest you hurry or your lunch will get cold."

# CHAPTER 6

"You can't quit, David," Jeremy pleaded with the instructor. "We need you. A lot of people come here expecting to learn to ski."

David Watts stood on the Parsonses' front porch staring at the floor. "I know the timing is bad, kid. But when your grandfather fired me yesterday I put out a few feelers. I was kind of surprised myself about how quickly I landed the job. The pay is real good and the hours aren't as long. I'd be a fool not to take it."

"I guess I understand." Jeremy leaned on the porch swing. "When are you leaving?"

"They want me to come as soon as I can. But I told them the situation here. The manager said I could have until the end of the week."

Jeremy extended his hand. "There's no hard feelings, David. I'll have my grandmother sign a check for you when she comes back."

The instructor took Jeremy's hand and shook it earnestly. "You're all right, kid. I hope things work out for you."

"Me too." Jeremy watched David disappear up the trail.

Jeremy's shoulders were drooping as he walked back into the house. Lila was dusting the furniture in the living room. "More bad news?"

Jeremy nodded and walked down the hall to his room. He gathered up all the paperwork, put it in the cardboard box, and carried it to the living room. "I'll be in my grandfather's office at the lodge if anyone needs me, Lila."

"You're taking on a lot of responsibility, Jeremy. Perhaps you should wait until your grand-mother—"

Jeremy let the screen door slam behind him. "Let me know if the hospital calls," he told Lila as he left.

The snow in front of the lodge had packed down and was icy and slick. Jeremy wondered why the staff hadn't put salt on it. His head hurt. He wondered about a lot of things lately. There was a lot more to running Thunder Valley than he had imagined.

Jeremy had barely sat down in his grandfather's big leather office chair when someone knocked frantically on the door.

"What now?" Jeremy pulled the door open. It was Hans, the stocky, middle-aged desk clerk.

"Your brother called on the red-line telephone from the ski lift on Sawtooth. The lift has jammed and there are people still in the chairs."

Jeremy grabbed his jacket. "Find Simms and send him up there. Alert the ski patrol and tell my brother I'm on my way." He took the keys to one of the lodge's snowmobiles and ran outside.

The Sawtooth lift was only minutes away. Jeremy could see a line of people impatiently waiting to get on the lift, which was swinging high above the ground with several pairs of ski boots dangling below the chairs.

Jeremy pulled up to the lift operation station. "What's going on?"

Chuck, the lift operator, shook his head. "It doesn't make sense. The darn thing just stopped. I can't seem to find anything wrong with it."

Jason put his hands in the air. "Don't look at me. All I know is the skiers are getting restless and we better get it going again real soon."

Jeremy could hear the people on the lift starting to yell and curse. He stepped away from the controls, shielded his eyes from the sun, and followed the cable route.

There it was. About ten feet down the cable something yellow was stuck in one of the pulleys.

"I see it, Chuck." Jeremy pointed at the problem.

"Oh, man." The operator wiped his greasy hands on his pants. "How did that get there?"

Jason stared up at the pulley. "A better question is, how are we gonna get it out of there?"

Jeremy moved to the end of the cable. "It's only about a ten- or fifteen-foot drop. I'm going to go after it."

Before anyone could stop him, Jeremy had

jumped up and grabbed the end of the cable. He worked his way across hand over hand. When he reached the pulley, he paused to rest. Then he let go with his left hand and tried to pull the yellow object free.

It wouldn't budge.

Jeremy's arms were getting tired. "Start the engine," he yelled at Chuck. "But keep it real slow."

Chuck ran to the controls. As the engine roared to life, Jeremy began tugging with all his might. Bit by bit, a long yellow scarf came untangled from the pulley.

With a jerk the lift started to move, and the people on the lift, as well as the crowd below, began clapping and cheering. Jeremy rode the cable to the end of the lift and lightly dropped to the ground with the scarf in his hand.

He held it up to Jason. "Recognize this?"

Jason looked confused. "It's my scarf. But how—"

"You didn't play another one of your practical jokes, did you?" Jeremy demanded.

"I've done a lot of dumb things, but I wouldn't put people in danger like this." Jason glanced from Chuck to Jeremy. "You believe me, don't you?"

Jeremy looked at the torn scarf. "I believe you. But we need to talk. If you've got a couple of minutes I want you to come down to the office with me. In my opinion, there have been a few too many *accidents* around here lately."

# CHAPTER 7

The desk clerk, Hans, met them at the front door of the lodge, obviously upset. "I've looked everywhere for the maintenance man but he just isn't to be found."

"Why doesn't this surprise me?" Jeremy sighed. "Keep trying to find him, Hans. When he does turn up, send him to my grandfather's office. I want to talk to him."

Jason cocked his head. "Hey, you sound like a natural-born administrator. Grandpa would be proud."

"Not if he heard about David Watts quitting."

Jason followed his brother into the comfortable office and closed the door. "I thought David *wanted* to work here."

"He did until he suddenly got a better job offer. And that's not all. Grandpa was right about the bank statements. Something's screwy."

"What do you think it is?"

"I don't know. But you and I better figure some things out before this whole place goes under."

There was a loud knock on the door. Jeremy yelled, "Come in," and an enormous, unshaven man with greasy brown hair sauntered into the room.

The man put his large hands on his hips and sneered at them. "You little boys shouldn't be playing around in your granddaddy's office. You might break something."

Jeremy ignored the comment. "Where have you been, Simms? I've had people looking for you. We had a problem on one of the lifts."

"Working. Where else would I be?"

Jeremy gritted his teeth. He was about to tell Simms off when he noticed something familiar on one of his hands. It was a tattoo of the same symbol that was on Corky's medallion.

Jason didn't wait. "My brother and I are in charge around here until our grandparents get back. So if you want to keep your job, I suggest you give us a straight answer."

Simms leaned over the desk and stared threateningly at the boys. "I don't work for no kids. If the old man has a problem with me, tell him to let me know in person." The big man turned and lumbered out of the office, slamming the door behind him.

"Are we just gonna take that?" Jason demanded.

Jeremy tapped the desk, deep in thought. "Jason, do you get the feeling that we're missing something? I don't know, maybe we're in over our heads."

"What are you talking about? That guy's not a problem. As soon as we get a chance to talk to Grandma, he's history."

Jeremy explained about the symbol he'd noticed. "The chances of two guys as different as Corky and Simms wearing that same emblem are probably about a million to one."

"You think those two are behind the problems the lodge has been having?"

"Who knows? One thing's for sure, we better stay on our toes. If there is a connection, we may be in for a lot more trouble."

Jason sat down on the other side of the desk and propped his feet up on it. "I sure will be glad when Grandma gets back. It was a lot more fun to just cruise around and enjoy myself on the slopes than it is running this place."

Jeremy frowned. "The thing is, we can't worry Grandma with any of this right now. She's got enough on her mind."

"Then what are we gonna do?"

"For now, just keep your eyes open. Everybody at the lodge is under suspicion. This thing could be bigger than we know."

# CHAPTER 8

"Would you mind paying attention, Mr. Parsons?"

Jeremy blinked. He was sitting at the dining room table and Mr. Stern, their tutor, was standing in front of him with a sour look on his face. "This era of ancient history is especially fascinating given our current archaeological data. In fact, I've been thinking of having you and your brother write a lengthy report discussing the implications of the latest findings."

Jason groaned and kicked his brother under the table.

Jeremy sat up straighter in his chair and tried

to collect his thoughts. "Sorry, Mr. Stern. I was thinking about something else."

"So I see." The tutor walked around the table and picked up the piece of notebook paper Jeremy had been doodling on during the lecture. "Mr. Parsons, you surprise me. Where exactly have you seen this sign before?" He held up the picture of the symbol Jeremy had drawn.

"Why?" Jeremy asked cautiously. "Do you know what it is?"

"My dear boy, as I've said before, my specialty is ancient history. Of course I know what it is. It's the symbol of a primitive pagan religion called the Broken Tree, which disappeared thousands of years ago. They were tree worshipers, very similar to the Druids, but with a twist. They only allowed the criminal element to join their ranks. Not just any criminals, mind you, only those with very special talents."

Jeremy was excited but tried not to show it. "Could there still be members of this Broken Tree thing around today?"

"That would be highly unlikely. Not in the truest sense, anyway."

"Mr. Stern." Lila was standing in the doorway. "I don't believe you should be filling the boys' heads with this sort of nonsense. Mrs. Parsons would be very upset if she knew."

"Quite right." The tutor cleared his throat. "Now, where were we . . . Oh, yes, page ninety-five."

The next two hours of tutoring dragged by for Jeremy. The information Mr. Stern had given him made it even more difficult to concentrate on his studies. What if there were actual members of this Broken Tree group working at the lodge?

Thankfully, the tutor let them go when a car pulled up outside. It was their grandmother. She had taken a cab from the city.

The woman who walked through the front door was not the same one who had left in the ambulance that morning. Grace Parsons was smiling and back in control. She assured her grandsons that their grandfather was out of danger and doing so well that he was already giving the nurses a hard time about the food. She had only come back to pack an overnight bag so that she could return to the hospital.

The boys were careful not to worry her with

any of the day's events, other than to explain about David Watts and to ask her to fill out a payroll check for him.

When she was through packing, Jeremy carried his grandmother's small suitcase to the waiting cab and deposited it in the open trunk.

Jeremy let his grandmother give him a parting hug as he opened the cab door for her. "Umm . . ." He hesitated, not sure how to ask her what he wanted to know. "Is Grandpa still depressed?"

"Depressed?" His grandmother raised an eyebrow. "Where on earth did you get that idea? It would take a lot more than accidentally taking the wrong medicine to depress your grandfather."

Jason came around the back of the cab. "But I thought Lila said—"

"You better go, Grandma," Jeremy interrupted. "The meter's running, and we know how impatient Grandpa gets."

Grace Parsons laughed. "That's putting it mildly." She hugged them both again and stepped into the cab. They waved until she was out of sight.

"All right, start talking," Jason ordered. "Why did Lila say those things about Grandpa if they weren't true?"

"Lower your voice," Jeremy whispered. He led his brother away from the house to a group of tall pine trees on the other side of the yard. When he was sure they were out of hearing range, he confided, "I don't understand it all yet. But I'm convinced that someone, or maybe even a lot of people, are trying to ruin Grandpa." He looked back at the house. "And now they're starting to play rough."

"Maybe we better call the cops."

"Do you think they'd believe us? We don't have much to go on. Besides, I'm pretty sure Lila listens on the extension."

"No problem." Jason rubbed his stomach. "Suddenly I feel very hungry. Don't worry, I'll keep her busy cooking for a while. You go into Grandpa's room and make the call."

# CHAPTER 9

Jason held his stomach as he closed the bedroom door. "Man, I'm hurting. For once in my life I think I overdid it. Tell me it was worth it."

Jeremy was sitting at the desk with a pencil and pad, trying to organize everything that had happened into some kind of logical order. He swung around and faced his brother. "We're not going to get any help from the cops. I called every agency in the phone book, including the FBI. The sheriff's department said they've never heard of the Broken Tree. The city police thought I was making a crank call. The FBI took my name but told me to have an adult call if an actual crime occurs." Jeremy shook his head. "It's no good. We're in this alone until we can come up with something solid for the police to go on." He stood and grabbed his coat from its peg.

"Where do you think you're going? It's ten o'clock at night."

"*We're* going up to the office to search the files. There's got to be a clue somewhere that can tell us why these things are happening, and we're gonna find it if it takes all night."

Jason moaned as he reached for his jacket. "I hope you realize what a sacrifice I'm making here."

Jeremy stuffed his notes into his pocket. "Some sacrifice. You'll probably be hungry again in an hour." He opened the door and stepped into the hall just in time to see Lila disappearing into the kitchen.

Jason saw too. "Do you think she was listening?"

"I don't know. But starting now, we better be a lot more careful."

# CHAPTER 10

Jason opened one eye. The yellow rays of the sun were just beginning to peek over the top of the snow-covered mountains. He raised his head off his grandfather's desk, where it had fallen a few hours earlier, yawned, and stretched as far as he could.

Jeremy was sitting in the middle of the floor going through a box of papers he'd found on the top shelf in the closet. "Have you ever heard Grandpa mention anything about Timothy Ryland Enterprises?"

Jason opened his other eye. "Have you been up all night?"

"Almost. Ever heard of it?"

"Nope."

"Me neither, but it could be something. This Ryland guy has made a couple of offers to buy the lodge. His company's in New York."

"Must not have meant much to Grandpa if he stuffed the offers in a box."

"You're probably right." Jeremy wrote down the address and phone number from one of the letters. "But just in case, I think I'll make some calls and see what I can find out."

Jason pushed himself away from the desk and stood up. "I'm starving. How about breakfast?"

"You go ahead. I'll get a doughnut or something later. After I clean up here, I'll make those calls and meet you over at the beginners' runs." He checked his watch. "It's two hours later in New York. I hope it's not too early."

He dialed the number and waited. A woman with a friendly, singsong voice answered. Before he could say anything she informed him that he'd reached an answering service and should leave a message. He decided to hang up without leaving one.

But then he thought again. He dialed the number again. He listened to the message, waited, and then spoke slowly, "This is the Thunder Valley Ski Lodge. We have found the Broken Tree."

# CHAPTER 11

Students young and old were starting to assemble for lessons on the flat beginners' area. The Thompson brothers were already pounding each other with snowballs when Jeremy arrived. For the sake of the rest of the class he decided to let Jason teach while he kept the troublemakers apart.

"Has everybody checked their bindings?" Jason asked. "Good, because we're going to work on something a little unusual today—falling down."

The oldest Thompson laughed. "What's so hard about that? I do it all the time."

"Believe it or not," Jason continued, "there is a right way to fall. Okay, everybody, let's try it. Bend your knees . . . more . . . more. Relax. Now we're all going to fall sideways and try to land on the seat of our pants. Ready . . . go."

The whole class was laughing. Everyone was sitting in the snow waiting for Jason's next instruction.

"There, that wasn't so bad. Now we're going to get up. Make sure your skis are close together. Bend those knees again and bring your hips as close as you can to your feet. Then use your poles to push yourself up. Okay, here we go."

With a little effort, almost every student managed to stand. All except one—Mr. Beardsley. He was an older man who was out of shape and more than slightly overweight. Try as he might, he just couldn't push hard enough to stand up.

"Do you mind if I offer a suggestion?" A tall, dark-haired man with a friendly face who had been watching from the sidelines stepped forward. "I've had a little practice with this sort of thing."

Jason shrugged. "Go ahead."

The man told Mr. Beardsley to roll onto his back, straighten out his skis, and swing back into position.

The heavyset man tried it, and to everyone's surprise, he succeeded in standing up.

Jason thanked the stranger and then went back to his lesson. Jeremy worked his way around to the man and offered his hand. "I'm Jeremy Parsons. My brother and I really appreciate your stepping in on that one."

"No problem." The man shook Jeremy's hand. "I'm Tom Caplan. I know what it's like to have a student in that predicament."

Jeremy's ears perked up. "You're a ski instructor?"

"I used to be. Right now I'm an out-of-work architect."

"Would you be interested in giving lessons here at Thunder Valley until you land a job?"

"I don't know." Tom Caplan scratched his head. "I really hadn't thought about anything like that."

48

"Don't say no yet. How about coming over to our house tonight and meeting my grandmother? She'll be home from the hospital tonight because my grandfather's doing much better. She does the actual hiring."

"Well, I—"

"What room are you staying in?" asked Jeremy. "I'll call you to let you know when she'll be home."

"I'm in twenty-three, but—"

"Great. Nice to meet you, Tom. And thanks again for your help." Jeremy moved back to the class.

"What was that all about?" Jason whispered.

Jeremy glanced back at Tom Caplan. "Let's just say that maybe things are finally starting to look up around here."

# CHAPTER 12

"There's a Mr. Ryland waiting for you in your grandfather's office." Hans came around the front desk and spoke to Jeremy in a low tone. "I told him that your grandfather was ill, but he insisted on speaking to you."

"It's all right, Hans. I want to talk to him."

Jeremy hurried across the lobby to the office and opened the door. A distinguished gray-haired man wearing a tailored black suit and a burgundy silk tie rose to meet him. "Mr. Jeremy Parsons?"

Jeremy nodded. "That's me. And you must be Timothy Ryland. What can I do for you?"

"I find myself in a rather awkward position, Jeremy. You see, your grandfather had agreed to meet with me today to discuss terms, and now I find he's in the hospital."

"What kind of terms?"

"Didn't he tell you? He has agreed to sell Thunder Valley to my company."

Jeremy slowly sat down in his grandfather's chair. "He didn't tell any of us. Probably because he changed his mind."

"I'm afraid that's not possible at this point." Timothy Ryland snapped open his briefcase and took out several papers. "These are all legal documents signed by your grandfather granting us ownership for the amount stated."

Jeremy studied the signature at the bottom of one of the papers. It was his grandfather's bold handwriting, all right. He didn't know what to say, so he stared out the window for a few minutes. "I'll have to speak to my grandmother about this, Mr. Ryland."

"Certainly. Perhaps there might be a conve-

nient time when I could speak with your grand-mother.''

"It's hard to say. I'll have her get in touch with you. Where are you staying?''

"Why, here, of course. I had assumed that the property would be changing hands this week.''

Jeremy walked to the door and held it open. "Like I said, I'll have her get in touch with you.''

Ryland put the papers back into his briefcase. "I'm sorry this came as such a shock to you, Jeremy.'' He moved to the door. "By the way, my answering service gave me a rather cryptic message this morning. They said the caller was from here but didn't leave his name. You don't know anything about it, do you?''

Jeremy tried to read the man's face. He seemed to be genuinely concerned.

"Sorry, Mr. Ryland. Can't help you.''

# CHAPTER 13

Jeremy sat numbly looking out the office window at all the people enjoying themselves in the snow. It was unbelievable that his grandfather could have done this thing. Thunder Valley was more than just a business. It was a way of life.

There was a tap on the door. Jeremy didn't answer. He didn't care who it was or what they wanted.

Hans poked his head into the office.

"Sorry to bother you, Jeremy. Your brother just called. He said something important has come up and for you to meet him as soon as you can at the snowmobile garage."

In a daze, Jeremy put his jacket on and walked down the road to the garage.

He found the garage door shut and locked, so he walked around to the smaller side door. It was standing wide open.

A noise came from the back of the garage, where extra parts were stored.

"Jason, is that you?"

There was no answer.

Jeremy slowly moved through the dark garage. There was a strange orange glow in the back. "Hello?"

A figure in black darted past him, knocking him backward into a tool chest.

Jeremy scrambled to his feet. Something didn't smell right.

Smoke!

He felt for the light switch on the wall and flipped it on. The room was half filled with thick black smoke. Frantically he tried to figure out where it was coming from. He dropped to his knees and searched.

The trash can. Flames had jumped from the small metal can to some rags lying near it and were licking at the wooden wall of the garage.

Jeremy took off his coat and tried beating at the fire. The flames almost gobbled up his nylon jacket. There was nothing else around to use and the smoke was getting worse.

Jeremy remembered the sink in the washroom. Grabbing a plastic tub from a hook on the wall, he ran and filled the tub with water. Moving as fast as he could in the choking smoke, he dumped tub after tub of water on the fire until the flames were completely out.

Exhausted, he made his way to the front of the building. The knob on the door turned but the door refused to open. He beat on it and called for help until his hoarse throat and aching lungs gave out.

Seconds ticked by. He was starting to feel dizzy. His eyes stung and each breath was ragged and painful. He dropped to his knees, trying not to lose consciousness.

Suddenly the door opened and a pair of strong hands pulled him out of the smoke-filled garage into the fresh air.

# CHAPTER 14

"Are you sure you're going to be all right?"

Jeremy nodded. He swung his legs off his grandmother's couch and sat up. "Thanks for everything, Tom. If you hadn't found me, I'd probably still be in the garage."

"I'm glad I happened along. Whoever left that snowmobile parked in front of the door like that should have known better."

"They probably did," Jeremy muttered.

"What?"

"Nothing. I was just agreeing with you."

The front door burst open and Jason rushed

in. "Why am I always the last one to hear about stuff? Hans told me you asked him to send someone to the garage to make sure the fire was completely out. What fire?"

Tom moved to the door. "Looks like I'm leaving you in good hands, Jeremy. I'll be in my room. Call if you need anything?"

"I will. Thanks again." When the door was closed, Jeremy put his feet back up on the couch.

"Well?" Jason asked impatiently. "What happened?"

Jeremy told him about the message Hans had given him.

"I never called you!" Jason exclaimed. "Somebody's pulling something here. I've been helping Chuck up at the ski lift all morning."

"I know that now. I'm pretty sure whoever left the message was also behind the fire."

"Then that means . . ."

"Right. They locked me in on purpose."

"Wow." Jason sat in the chair across from Jeremy. "Maybe it's time to try the cops again. If Tom hadn't come along, you'd be *dead*."

"What good would it do? We don't have any

proof. Whoever's responsible is pretty good at making things look like accidents."

"Yeah. It's almost like someone wants Grandpa to sell out."

"That's what I thought too. Until this morning when I found out he already has."

Jason looked confused. "What are you talking about?"

"It's true. A man named Ryland came to the office and showed me some papers. Grandpa has already sold the lodge."

"There has to be some kind of mistake! He would have told us."

"I saw the signature," Jeremy said quietly.

"I don't care what you saw. This Ryland guy's playing with our heads. Where's Lila?"

"She went to town for groceries. Why?"

Jason jumped to his feet and stormed out of the room. "She's been flaky right from the start. If anybody knows something about this, it's her. I'd bet money on it."

"Wait. What are you going to do?" Jeremy followed his brother down the hall.

Jason threw open the door of Lila's room. The bed was made and everything was neat as a pin.

He looked inside her closet. Several drab house-dresses hung from the rack. Two suitcases stood on the floor near the back. He hauled them out. The first one was empty. He shoved it back and pulled out the second one. It was locked.

"Here. Try this." Jeremy handed him his pocketknife.

Jason wiggled it around until he finally forced the lock open. Inside was a strange assortment of wigs and makeup. He took out a long blond wig. "What do you make of this?"

"Looks like Lila's not all she pretends to be." Jeremy went to the dresser. On top was a small jewelry case. He flipped it open. Inside was a diamond wedding ring resting on a red velvet pillow. But it wasn't the ring that caught his eye. Gently he pulled out a gold chain and held it up for Jason to see.

Hanging from the chain was the emblem of the Broken Tree.

# CHAPTER 15

"Are you sure we left everything in her room the way it was?" Jeremy asked. "Until we get to the bottom of this, the last thing we want to do is make Lila suspicious."

"For the tenth time, I'm sure." Jason stopped his brother a few feet in front of the lodge. "What I'm worried about is this Ryland guy. Maybe we should wait for a better time."

"Hey, don't get cold feet on me now. You're the one who thought of this. You said there might be a connection between the buyer and the rest of this Broken Tree group. Besides, there may not be a better time to search his room. While he's at lunch we'll make a quick search. All we need is one tiny piece of evidence that he's in on it."

Jason frowned. "What if I'm wrong? Lila is one thing, but a big-time New York businessman is another."

"Think of it this way. If the guy's innocent we need to know so we can look somewhere else."

Jason followed him up the steps and inside the lodge. "I hope you're right."

"Right about what?" Tom Caplan came up behind them.

Jeremy tried to cover. "Jason was just wondering if I should be up and around after what happened this morning. I told him I was feeling great."

"Glad to hear it. Say, I was just on my way to lunch. Would you guys like to join me?"

Jason licked his lips.

"No, thank you." Jeremy grabbed his brother's sleeve and led him across the room to the front desk. "We have to check on something. Maybe some other time."

Jeremy moved around behind the front desk

and pretended to look at the reservations book. "How's everything going, Hans?" he asked the desk clerk.

"Booked solid, as usual. I've had to turn away three callers this morning alone."

"Really? That's too bad." Jeremy checked to see which room was Timothy Ryland's and then winked at Jason, who accidentally on purpose knocked a pen-and-pencil holder onto the floor. When Hans bent down to retrieve it, Jeremy grabbed the key to Ryland's room and moved around the counter.

"Sorry about that, Hans." Jason checked to make sure nothing was broken and then caught up with Jeremy, who was already halfway down the hall. "What room is he in?"

"We're in luck. He's on the first floor, room five."

Jeremy walked up to the door and knocked loudly. There was no answer. He glanced over his shoulder. "Ready?"

"As I'll ever be."

Jeremy inserted the key. They hurried inside and quickly closed the door.

"You take the closet and the bed," Jeremy instructed. "I'll check the dresser and the bath-room."

Jason opened the closet. There was nothing suspicious about the suits and shoes. Ryland's suitcase was empty. Jason moved to the bed and searched underneath it and between the mat-tresses.

Jeremy stepped out of the bathroom. "I didn't find anything. Did you?"

Jason shook his head. "No. Maybe he's what he claims to be after all."

Jeremy snapped his fingers. "The briefcase. He had a briefcase earlier."

The door swung open. "You don't mean *this* briefcase, do you?" Ryland stepped into the room holding a black case. Corky and Simms blocked the doorway behind him.

"I guess you two think you're pretty clever, don't you?" Ryland looked thoughtful. "In a way, I suppose I do have to give you credit. Detectives in three different states haven't caught on to us. You've actually come closer than anyone. Not that it'll do you any good when Simms is through with you."

Jeremy inched back toward the bathroom

door. When Jason saw what he was doing he tried to keep Ryland talking. "So where's Lila? Your Broken Tree gang isn't complete without her, is it?"

Ryland laughed. "So you know about my darling wife. She was very useful in switching your grandfather's medicine. In fact, Lila's at the hospital right now, talking your grandmother into coming home. We need her signature to transfer ownership of Thunder Valley to our organization."

Jeremy was almost to the bathroom door. Jason went on talking. "I thought you said my grandfather already signed the papers."

"That was a forgery. An excellent one, I might add, done by your friend Corky. But a forgery nonetheless. We're after the real thing. Our plan has always been to have the old lady sign the necessary papers. Of course she won't know what she's signing. But after all these terrible accidents, including the one you two are about to have, we think she'll be glad to get rid of it."

Jeremy bolted into the bathroom and locked the door.

"Get him, Simms!" Ryland yelled.

Simms slammed his body into the door until it came off its hinges in splinters. The small window above the tub was open.

The bathroom was empty.

# CHAPTER 16

Jeremy ran for the woods behind the lodge. He had to think, figure out what to do. They desperately needed help, but who could give it to them? If he could just get to a telephone, maybe there would be a deputy sheriff in the area.

He stayed in the cover of the trees and crept toward the back porch. Silently he inched up the steps, opened the screen door, and listened. The house was quiet.

Jeremy raced down the hall to his grandfather's bedroom and dialed 911. A female dispatcher came on the line.

"Calm down, son. Tell me the problem. Is anyone hurt?"

Jeremy tried to catch his breath. "My brother . . . they have my brother . . . hurry."

"Who has your brother?"

"Some people." Jeremy's mind raced. "Kidnappers. Come to the Thunder Valley Ski Lodge, and hurry."

He heard the sound of a telephone being quietly hung up in another part of the house. "Hurry!" he yelled. Dropping the receiver, he tore around the bed.

"Not so fast."

Jeremy froze. Lila stood in the door pointing a small silver pistol at him. "Sounds like it's a good thing I came back. You and your twin brother have caused enough trouble. We should have gotten rid of you a long time ago."

"Where's my grandmother?" Jeremy demanded.

"Oh, she's on her way. But don't worry, we'll have you safely out of the picture before she gets here."

"Give me the gun, Mrs. Ryland."

Jeremy couldn't believe his eyes. Tom Caplan, along with several other men, was standing behind Lila. The tall man moved up and took the gun out of her hand. "Put the cuffs on her, boys, and take her away."

Lila's shoulders slumped. She gave up without a struggle. Jeremy stepped back to give Tom room. "Are you a cop?"

Tom smiled. "Undercover. We've been after this group for years. They move in on unsuspecting businesses and cause enough unexplained accidents to make the owners want to sell. Until now we haven't been able to prove anything. But thanks to you and your brother, I think we have them this time."

"Jason! They've got him!"

"He's fine. Hans has already seen to that. And we have Ryland and his buddies in custody."

"Hans?" Jeremy followed Tom down the hall.

"He works for us. The day we received word that the Broken Tree was after the Thunder Valley Lodge, Hans applied for a job here."

Jeremy stopped on the front porch. "I don't get it. How did you know I was at the house?"

"We've been monitoring your actions for quite some time. When we saw you go into Ryland's room we put everybody on alert. It actually worked perfectly, your getting away from them like that. It confused things long enough for Hans to move in."

A black car pulled up in front of the house. Jason jumped out. "This is so great!" he yelled. "There are cops all over this place!"

Tom smiled again. "I'm glad everything's worked out. I'll be getting in touch with both of you as soon as I get these goons behind bars."

"Maybe then you could come back for a real vacation," Jeremy said. "On the house, of course."

"I'd like that. But only on one condition— that you let me bring a friend along."

"Sure." Jason nodded. "Bring anyone you want."

"Good. I've been telling Jean-Claude about this place. He's been wanting to come up ever since he heard about the big race with Jeremy up on Sawtooth." Tom stepped into the car. "I'll be in touch."

Jeremy's mouth fell open. He watched the black car pull out of the driveway and join three others waiting beside the road.

Jason waved and then turned toward the house. "All this excitement's made me hungry. Want a sandwich?"

"You don't think he meant *the* Jean-Claude, do you?" Jeremy asked.

Jason shrugged. "Why not? As an undercover agent, Tom probably gets around. He may know a lot of famous people. Hey, where are you going? Aren't you hungry?"

"I've got more important things to do." Jeremy jumped up onto the porch and ran inside the house.

"Like what?" Jason yelled.

When Jeremy reappeared he was smiling and carrying his skis. "Practicing. I've got a race to win."

# GARY PAULSEN
## ADVENTURE GUIDE

### SKI GUIDE

**Who is Jean-Claude Killy?** Jean-Claude Killy is mentioned in this story a couple of times. He's a world-famous skier, born in France in 1943. He won all three Alpine skiing events—the downhill, the slalom, and the giant slalom—at the 1968 Winter Olympics. He also won World Cup titles in 1967 and 1968.

#### Ski Safety Tips

- If you've never skied before, you should take a lesson from a professional ski instructor.
- Dress in layers of clothing to keep warm. That way, if you get too hot while you're skiing, you can take a layer off. Don't forget to wear a hat! Wear a waterproof or water-resistant layer over your clothes to keep dry.
- Wear ski goggles or sunglasses with ultraviolet protection.
- Make sure your boots fit correctly, your skis are the right length for you, and your bindings are adjusted properly.
- Practice putting your skis on and taking them off before you start skiing.

- If you're cross-country skiing, always stay on the marked trails.
- Be safe while you're skiing by following these rules:

    Don't ski too fast—you might lose control.

    Avoid other skiers.

    Don't block trails.

    Yield when merging with other skiers.

    Observe all signs.

### *Brrrrrr!*

If you don't wear proper clothing while skiing, you might suffer from *frostbite* (loss of feeling in your body parts) or *hypothermia* (low body temperature). If you get frostbite, you should go inside immediately and seek medical attention as soon as possible. Tuck numb hands under your armpits beneath your coat, and cover a frostbitten face with dry gloved hands until normal color returns. *Do not rub* or use direct heat on frostbitten body parts.

For hypothermia, you should gradually and gently rewarm your body. If you're stuck outdoors for some reason, huddle with another person or hold your knees to your chest and wrap your arms around your legs.

### Helping Other Skiers

If you see an injured skier, don't move him or her. Remove your own skis and stick them in the snow upright and crossed to form an X about ten feet up the hill from the person who is hurt. This X warns other skiers to stay clear and alerts the ski patrol to your location. Send another skier for help or consult your trail map for the closest emergency phone.

**Don't miss all the exciting action!**

### The Legend of Red Horse Cavern

Will Little Bear Tucker and his friend Sarah Thompson have heard the eerie Apache legend many times. Will's grandfather especially loves to tell them about Red Horse—an Indian brave who betrayed his people, was beheaded, and now haunts the Sacramento Mountain range, searching for his head. To Will and Sarah it's just a story—until they decide to explore a new-found mountain cave, a cave filled with danger-ous treasures.

Deep underground, Will and Sarah uncover an old chest stuffed with a million dollars. But now armed bandits are after them. When they find a gold Apache statue hidden in a skull, it seems Red Horse is hunting them, too. Then they lose their way, and each step they take in the damp, dark cavern could be their last.

### Rodomonte's Revenge

Friends Brett Wilder and Tom Houston are video game whizzes. So when a new virtual re-ality arcade called Rodomonte's Revenge opens near their home, they make sure they're its first customers. The game is awesome. There are flaming fire rivers to jump, beastly buzz-bugs to fight, and ugly tunnel spiders to escape. If they're good enough they'll face Rodomonte, an evil giant waiting to do battle within his hidden castle.

But soon after they play the game, strange things start happening to Brett and Tom. The computer is taking over their minds. Now everything that happens in the game is happening in real life. A buzz-bug could gnaw off their ears. Rodomonte could smash them to bits. Brett and Tom have no choice but to play Rodomonte's Revenge again. This time they'll be playing for their lives.

### *Escape from Fire Mountain*

*". . . please, anybody . . . fire . . . need help."*

That's the urgent cry thirteen-year-old Nikki Roberts hears over the CB radio the weekend she's left alone in her family's hunting lodge. The message also says that the sender is trapped near a bend in the river. Nikki knows it's dangerous, but she has to try to help. She paddles her canoe downriver, coming closer to the thick black smoke of the forest fire with each stroke. When she reaches the bend, Nikki climbs onshore. There, covered with soot and huddled on a rock ledge, sit two small children.

Nikki struggles to get the children to safety. Flames roar around them. Trees splinter to the ground. But as Nikki tries to escape the fire, she doesn't know that two poachers are also hot on her trail. They fear that she and the children have seen too much of their illegal operation—and they'll do anything to keep the kids from making it back to the lodge alive.

### The Rock Jockeys

*Devil's Wall.*

Rick Williams and his friends J.D. and Spud—the Rock Jockeys—are attempting to become the first and youngest climbers to ascend the north face of their area's most treacherous mountain. They're also out to discover if a B-17 bomber rumored to have crashed into the mountain years ago is really there.

As the Rock Jockeys explore Devil's Wall, they stumble upon the plane's battered shell. Inside, they find items that seem to have belonged to the crew, including a diary written by the navigator. Spud later falls into a deep hole and finds something even more frightening: a human skull and bones. To find out where they might have come from, the boys read the navigator's story in the diary. It reveals a gruesome secret that heightens the dangers the mountain might hold for the Rock Jockeys.

### Hook 'Em, Snotty!

Bobbie Walker loves working on her grandfather's ranch. She hates the fact that her cousin Alex is coming up from Los Angeles to visit and will probably ruin her summer. Alex can barely ride a horse and doesn't know the first thing about roping. There is no way Alex can survive a ride into the flats to round up wild cattle. But Bobbie is going to have to let her tag along anyway.

Out in the flats the weather turns bad. Even worse, Bobbie knows that she'll have to watch out for the Bledsoe boys, two mischievous brothers who are usually up to no good. When the boys rustle the girls' cattle, Bobbie and Alex team up to teach the Bledsoes a lesson. But with the wild bull Diablo on the loose, the fun and games may soon turn deadly serious.

### Danger on Midnight River

Daniel Martin doesn't want to go to Camp Eagle Nest. He wants to spend the summer as he always does: with his uncle Smitty in the Rocky Mountains. Daniel is a slow learner, but most other kids call him retarded. Daniel knows that at camp, things are only going to get worse. His nightmare comes true when he and three bullies must ride the camp van together.

On the trip to camp, Daniel is the butt of the bullies' jokes. He ignores them and concentrates on the roads outside. He thinks they may be lost. As the van crosses a wooden bridge, the planks suddenly give way. The van plunges into the raging river below. Daniel struggles to shore, but the driver and the other boys are nowhere to be found. It's freezing, and night is setting in. Daniel faces a difficult decision. He could save himself . . . or risk everything to try to rescue the others, too.

### The Gorgon Slayer

Eleven-year-old Warren Trumbull has a strange job. He works for Prince Charming's Damsel in Distress Rescue Agency, saving people from hideous monsters, evil warlocks, and wicked witches. Then one day Warren gets the most dangerous assignment of all: He must exterminate a Gorgon.

Gorgons are horrible creatures. They have green scales, clawed fingers, and snakes for hair. They also have the power to turn people to stone. Warren doesn't want to be a stone statue for the rest of his life. He'll need all his courage and skill—and his secret plan—to become a true Gorgon slayer.

The Gorgon howls as Warren enters the dark basement to do battle. Warren lowers his eyes, raises his sword and shield, and leaps into action. But will his plan work?

## Captive!

Roman Sanchez is trying hard to deal with the death of his dad—a SWAT team member gunned down in the line of duty. But Roman's nightmare is just beginning.

When masked gunmen storm into his classroom, Roman and three other boys are taken hostage. They are thrown into the back of a truck and hauled to a run-down mountain cabin, miles from anywhere. They are bound with rope and given no food. With each passing hour the kidnappers' deadly threats become even more real.

Roman knows time is running out. Now he must somehow put his dad's death behind him so that he and the others can launch a last desperate fight for freedom.

## The Treasure of El Patrón

Tag Jones and his friend Cowboy spend their days diving in the azure water surrounding Bermuda. It's not just for fun—Tag knows that somewhere in the coral reef there's a sunken ship full of treasure. His father died in a diving accident looking for the ship, and Tag won't give up until he finds it.

Then the ship's manifest of the Spanish galleon *El Patrón* turns up, and Tag can barely contain his excitement. *El Patrón* sank in 1614, carrying "unknown cargo." Tag knows that *this* is the ship his father was looking for. And he's not the least bit scared off by the rumors that *El Patrón* is cursed. But when two tourists want Tag to retrieve some mysterious sunken parcels for them, Tag and Cowboy may be in dangerous water, way over their heads!

### Skydive!

Jesse Rodriguez has a pretty exciting job for a thirteen-year-old, working at a small flight and skydiving school near Seattle. Buck Sellman, the owner of the school, lets Jesse help out around the airport and is teaching him all about skydiving. Jesse can't wait until he's sixteen and old enough to make his first jump.

Then Robin Waterford walks in with her father one day to sign up for lessons, and strange things start to happen. Photographs that Robin takes of the airfield mysteriously disappear from her locker. And Robin and Jesse discover that someone at the airfield is involved in an illegal transportation operation. Jesse and Robin soon find themselves in the middle of real danger and are forced to make their first skydives very unexpectedly—using only one parachute!

### The Seventh Crystal

*Chosen One,*
*The ancient palace lies in the Valley of Zon. It is imperative that you come immediately. You are my last hope. Look for the secret path. The*

*stars will lead the way. Take care. The eyes of Mogg are everywhere.*

As if school bullies weren't enough of a problem, now Chris Masters has a computer game pushing him around! Ever since The Seventh Crystal arrived anonymously in the mail one day, Chris has been obsessed with it—it's the most challenging game he's ever played. But when the game starts to take over, Chris is forced to face a lean, mean, *medieval* bully.

### The Creature of Black Water Lake

Thirteen-year-old Ryan Swanner and his mom just moved to the mountain resort of Black Water Lake. The locals say that beneath the lake's seemingly calm surface, a giant, ancient creature lives. But Ryan's new friend Rita tells him that's just hogwash. She's not afraid to go fishing out on the lake, even though, oddly, the lake seems to be nearly empty of fish. One day Ryan sees a small animal fall from a tree into the lake—and never surface again. Something *is* in the lake. And it's alive. . . .

### Time Benders

Superbrain Zack Griffin and hoops fanatic Jeff Brown wouldn't normally hang together. But when both boys win trips to a famous science laboratory, they find out they have one thing in common: a serious case of curiosity. And when they sneak into the lab to check out the time-bending machine again, they end up in Egypt—in 1350 B.C.!

### Grizzly

Justin swallowed and pointed the light at the soft dirt. The tracks were plain: two large pads with five long scissorlike claws on each.

*A grizzly.*

A grizzly bear is terrorizing the sheep ranch that belongs to Justin McCallister's aunt and uncle. First the grizzly takes a swipe at the ranch's guard dog, Old Molly. Then he kills several sheep and injures Justin's collie, Radar. When the grizzly kills Blue, Justin's pet lamb, Justin decided to take matters into his own hands. He sets out to track down the bear himself. But what will Justin do when he comes face to face with the grizzly?